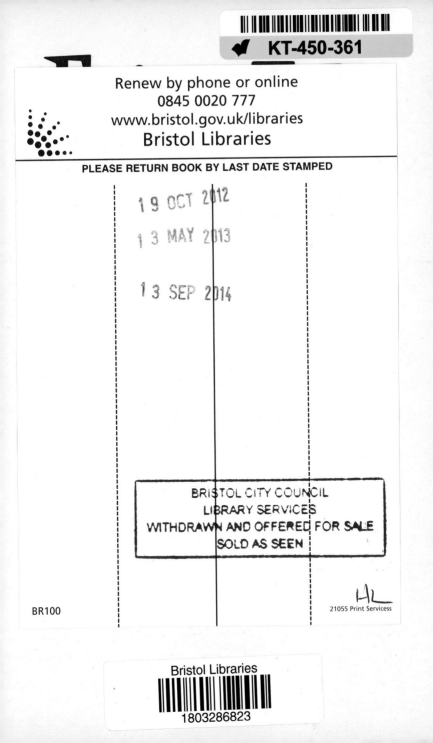

KT-450-361

Renew by phone or online
0845 0020 777
www.bristol.gov.uk/libraries
Bristol Libraries

PLEASE RETURN BOOK BY LAST DATE STAMPED

1 9 OCT 2012

1 3 MAY 2013

1 3 SEP 2014

BR100

21055 Print Servicess

For my wonderful Grandad, Charles,
and for Chris, my very own
Prince Charming x
K.D.

For Dad
M.B.

Reading Consultant: Prue Goodwin, Lecturer in literacy and children's books

ORCHARD BOOKS
338 Euston Road, London NW1 3BH
Orchard Books Australia
Level 17/207 Kent Street, Sydney, NSW 2000

First published in 2012
First paperback publication in 2013

ISBN 978 1 40831 214 8 (hardback)
ISBN 978 1 40831 222 3 (paperback)

A CIP catalogue record for this book is available
from the British Library.

1 3 5 7 9 10 8 6 4 2 (hardback)
1 3 5 7 9 10 8 6 4 2 (paperback)

Printed in Great Britain

Orchard Books is a division of Hachette Children's Books,
an Hachette UK company.

www.hachette.co.uk

Fairy Tale
Twists

Prince Charming's
Princess Quest

Written by Katie Dale
Illustrated by Matt Buckingham

ORCHARD

"Charming, dear," his mother said.
"We think it's time that you got wed.
The clock is ticking, son, and we're
not getting any younger, dear!
Go out and find a nice princess
– here, check the latest *In Distress* –
but if you do not," warned his mother,
"then the crown goes to your brother!"

The princesses were big and small
and fair and dark, and short and tall.
Some were bald and some were hairy,
one was even downright scary!

"Oh crumbs!" he wailed, and then he
   saw her:
blonde and beautiful Aurora.
Doomed to sleep till she was kissed.
The prince was helpless to resist!

He travelled far, through wind and
   hail...

Through wood and mountain, hill
   and dale...

Until at last he found the place,
and gazed upon her lovely face.

Prince Charming knelt down by her side,
and leant towards his future bride.
His eyes were closed, his lips were glossed,
Aurora woke...

And screamed, "**GET LOST!**
Just what d'ya think you're doing, chum?
Oh, wait a minute, hang on – Mum!
Another bloomin' prince!" she said,
then pulled the quilt over her head.

"I'm sorry, chuck," said Rora's mum,
"I know how far you must've come.
You must think we're a little crazy,

but my daughter's just so LAZY!
All she does is snooze and snore –
she never does a single chore!
I just asked her to spin this thread,
but no – she fell asleep instead!
I thought if I could get her wed
she'd *have* to leave her bloomin' bed!"

Charming bid them both goodbye,
and climbed his horse and gave a sigh.
"What now?" he thought. "I'll be in strife
if I return without a wife!"
He scanned the pictures, checked the list –
another maiden to be kissed!

"Well, if at first you don't succeed…"
thought Charming, spurring on his steed.

Her skin was white as fallen snow,
her lips like rubies seemed to glow.
Charming bent to kiss them – when
he saw a group of little men.

"She's dead!" one sobbed. "I'm sorry, mate,
it seems you've turned up just too late.
She ate the poisoned apple, see?"
Smiled Charming, "Leave it up to me."

He kissed her softly, held his breath…
but still the maiden lay like death!
He tried again, and twice and thrice,
but still her skin was cold as ice!

He cried, "There must be some mistake –
at True Love's Kiss she's meant to wake!"

"You mean it's just a spell?" Doc said.
"Snow White here isn't really dead?"
Another said – "Excuse me, mate,
But hang on, let me get this straight,
you say she's your true love, but yet,
you're telling me you've never met?"

"Well, no," said Charming, "but you see,
it's obvious – we're meant to be!
I'm bound to love her – it's my duty:
I'm a prince and she's a beauty!"

"Duty? Pah!" the dwarf replied.
"Excuse me, pal, please step aside."
You wanna see a True Love Kiss?"
He stood on tiptoes. "Just watch this."

Scoffed Charming, "It'll never work –
you're not a prince!" He hid his smirk.
But then to everyone's surprise…

The maiden woke and blinked her eyes!

"My love!" she cried in joyful song.
"I knew it was you all along!
We've wasted time, no more delay.
Let's marry, darling, right away!"

Charming sighed. "For pity's sake.
I'll find a princess who's awake!"
He scanned the page. "Well, who's
    that there?
The girl with all the golden hair?
Her name's Rapunzel – very queer –
at Bluebeard's Castle – ooh, that's near!"

So Charming set off for the tower
and arrived within the hour.

"Oh help me, please!" Rapunzel cried.
"A witch has locked me up inside!"

The fearless prince began to climb.
Alas! The walls were thick with slime!
As Charming's feet began to slip,
he felt his fingers lose their grip!
He slipped and slithered down the wall,
then grabbed a rope to break his fall.

"**OWW!**" Rapunzel cried. "You dope!"
"Get off my plait – it's not a rope!"
"Oh crumbs!" cried Charming, letting go,
and tumbling to the ground below.

"I'll never get you out!" he cried.
"Just knock the door down, dear,"
    she sighed.
The door caved in and she was free!
"My love!" cried Charming. "Marry me!"

"I'm grateful, sure," Rapunzel said.
"But do we really have to wed?
I want to see the world," she sighed.
"For so long I've been locked inside."

Charming sighed, then smiled. "Of course."
He even let her take his horse.

He watched her go, then, feeling glum,
he wandered home to face his mum.

The queen said, "You've got one
  more chance –
I have arranged a royal dance –
all the maidens in the land
will vie to win your royal hand."

Charming sighed. His feet were sore,
and speed-dating was such a bore.
But still, he might just find The One.
The queue of them went on and on…

…and on and on! But then he saw
a maiden in the corridor…
Instead of queuing up, this maid
was dancing as the music played.

Her style was certainly unique.
(A girl beside him muttered, "Freak!")
But something in her made him smile.
Perhaps this ball had been worthwhile...

She danced like there was no one there,
she clicked her heels and tossed her hair,
she clapped her hands and danced a storm.
Prince Charming felt his cheeks grow warm.

He watched her as if in a trance,
then took her hand and joined the dance.
They whirled and swirled and then
   they twirled:
the only people in the world.

The music stopped, but still they danced
and held each other close, entranced.
"You're great," sighed Charming as
    they spinned.
"You're not so bad yourself," she grinned.
"I love to dance, especially since
I know I'll never meet the prince."

The prince stopped dancing. "Sorry, what?
You'll never meet the prince? Why not?"

The maiden smiled. "I'm not a fool –
I'm not a beauty, I'm not cool,
my feet are huge, my hips are wide –
I'd hardly make a royal bride."

"Just look around at all these girls,
their dainty feet and golden curls.
My eyes don't match, my hair
    grows wild.
I've even hairy toes," she smiled.

"I don't fit in, but that's OK,
I'd rather boogie anyway.
Besides, if I were in that queue
I never would have danced with you."

Charming blushed, then shook his head.
"I think you're very wrong," he said.
"The prince, if he had half a clue,
would ditch the rest and marry you."

The maiden smiled, her cheeks aflame:
"But I don't even know your name."
"First tell me yours," the prince replied.
"My name is—"

      "**Charming!**" someone cried.

The queen rushed over. "Charming, dear!
Whatever are you doing here?"
"*You're* the prince?" the maiden said.
Her cheeks grew pink and then she fled.

"Come back!" cried Charming. "Stop
   her, wait!"
Alas, his cries had come too late.
He ran outside, but she had gone.
"I have to find her – she's The One!"

"I can help!" A girl appeared.
"Before your maiden disappeared
I saw her run across the grass
and drop this slipper made of glass."

"That's it!" cried Charming. "That's
    my clue!
I'll wed the girl who fits this shoe!"

The news spread quickly, far and wide,
as Charming hunted for his bride.
Crowds of women filled the street,
all offering their sweaty feet.

He made his way along the queue
but no one's foot would fit the shoe.
Some had warts and some had bunions,
one smelt just like cheese and onions!

Charming sighed and held his nose –
then spied a foot with hairy toes...

"My love!" cried Charming. "What's
   your name?"
The maiden beamed, her cheeks aflame.
"Don't laugh," she blushed. "My name
   is Belle."
He smiled. "A name that suits you well.
Oh Belle!" he cried. "It's really you!
Now quickly, love, put on your shoe."

"My shoe?" she frowned. "Prince
   Charming, wait—"
But Charming quickly grabbed a crate.
He held the shoe. "Now darling, sit."
He held his breath…

...It didn't fit!

Charming stared. "It cannot be!"

"This shoe does not belong to me –
I tried to tell you!" Bella sighed.

"Ooh, me next!" Cinderella cried.

She grabbed the shoe, brushed off the soot,
and slipped the slipper on her foot...

"A perfect fit!" King Henry cried.
"My dear, you'll make a lovely bride!"
"There's been a mix-up!" Charming said,
"I choose to marry Belle instead!"

"But Charming, darling, it was you
who said, 'Whoever fits the shoe' –
and look, it fits her foot so snugly.
(Plus her sister's really ugly!)"

"I don't care," Prince Charming said,
"*Belle's* the girl I'm going to wed."
Just then the ground began to shake.
Said Cind, "You've made a BIG mistake!"
The sky grew dark with thick black smoke
and from the cloud a woman spoke:

"Who dares to cross my magic schemes,
and ruin my goddaughter's dreams?
Who among you is it? Speak!"
"Um, me," gulped Charming, feeling weak.

She glared at Charming. "How absurd!
How dare you break your royal word,
and shun my darling Cinderella?
I don't think so – take that, fella!"
She waved her wand and in a flash
Prince Charming broke out in a rash.

She muttered curses dark and scary.
Charming's arms grew big and hairy…

He crumpled over on all fours,
his fingers curled up into claws.
His ears ballooned – the queen turned pale,
as Charming grew a bushy tail!

"That'll teach you," Fairy sneered,
then flicked her wand and disappeared.
The footmen stared, King Henry swore,
the queen fell flat upon the floor!

"Call the coach!" King Henry cried.
He grabbed the queen and jumped inside.
"Goodbye then all, so long, farewell!
Oh, Cinderella – come as well.
You'll marry Charming's little brother –
that should please your cross godmother.
You'll be queen when we are dead."
"OK then," Cinderella said.

"But hang on, Dad!" Prince Charming
  cried.

"What about my future bride?"

"I'm sorry, son, but understand,

a...*beast* could never rule this land!

You had your chance, you missed your cue,

now who will ever marry you?"

Poor Charming sighed and watched
  them go.
"Of course," he wailed. "He's right, I know.
I'm hideous! Just look at me –
no wonder they all scream and flee!
I've lost my fortune, lost my throne –
I'm bound to live my life alone!"

Belle replied, "You silly twit,
you're not as pretty, I'll admit,
but that's a blessing, don't you see?
Your life is yours at last – you're free!
No more duty, no more laws,
do what you want – the choice is yours!

"Now let your hair down, have some fun,
shout out loud, and laugh and run,
drive a train, race motor boats...

Keep a herd of billy goats...

Fight with snowballs, bathe in mud,
things that princes never could.

Who cares about those other things –
looks and money, queens and kings?
I love you just for being you."
Said Charming, "Is that really true?"
"Of course!" she smiled. "You
    dunder-head!"
So Belle and Charming promptly wed.

They filled their days with fun
    and laughter –
and both lived happily ever after.

Fairy Tale Twists

Written by Katie Dale
Illustrated by Matt Buckingham

The Big Bad Werewolf	978 1 40831 218 6
Goldilocks and the Pea	978 1 40831 219 3
The Not-So-Evil Stepmother	978 1 40831 220 9
The Wickedest Witch	978 1 40831 221 6
Prince Charming's Princess Quest	978 1 40831 222 3
The Unfair-y Godmother	978 1 40831 223 0
Jack to the Rescue!	978 1 40831 224 7
Three Magic Mice	978 1 40831 225 4

All priced at £4.99

Orchard Books are available from all good bookshops,
or can be ordered from our website, www.orchardbooks.co.uk,
or telephone 01235 827702, or fax 01235 827703.